The Silver o Balloon o
and other stories

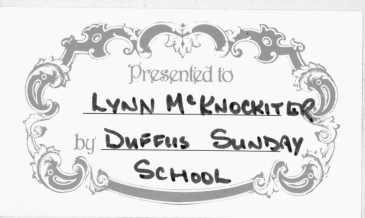

The Silver o Balloon o

and other stories

KATHLEEN CRAWFORD

Illustrated by Carolyn Crory

Scripture Union
130, City Road, London EC1V 2NJ

By the same author
Christopher's Band

© Kathleen Crawford 1988
First published 1988

ISBN 0 86201 493 X

Phototypeset by Input Typesetting Ltd., London
SW19 8DR
Printed and bound in Great Britain by Cox and
Wyman Ltd., Reading

Contents

For Sarah

The silver balloon

Every autumn, a fair came to the big city where Katie and her family lived. Daddy had promised that they could all go and see it when he came home from work. Katie could hardly wait. She was so excited that, when she tried to fasten her duffle coat, the loops got twisted and the toggles got mixed up, so that one side of her coat ended up looking longer than the other.

'Here, let me help you,' said Mummy, and fastened it properly for her.

As the bus arrived at the fairground Katie shouted, 'Look, there it is, over there, I can see the fair!' Through the trees they could see the bright lights twinkling and flashing against the dark sky. The big wheel was spinning round and round like a giant Catherine Wheel firework. As they came nearer, the noise of the fair became louder. Katie could hear the loud music, the clanging of bells and the roar of the engines which made the roundabouts work.

There were people everywhere. Some were laughing and chattering excitedly as they walked along. Others were shrieking and screaming as the rides they were on went faster and faster. Katie was not sure if that was because the people were frightened or happy. She held her mummy's hand tightly so that she did not fall over. It had been raining and the muddy ground squelched as they walked. Sarah, Katie's little sister, rode on Daddy's shoulders.

'Look at those,' said Katie excitedly. A man was holding the biggest bunch of balloons that she had ever seen. There were red ones, blue ones, yellow ones, white glittery ones and silver ones. Katie liked the silver ones best because they sparkled under the lights.

'Please can I have one?' she asked.

'Perhaps,' smiled Daddy, 'but not just yet. The balloon might burst when you go on the roundabouts.'

They stopped at a stall which sold food. Daddy bought some hot dogs and mushy peas with mint sauce, a toffee apple for Katie and a lollipop for Sarah. Katie could smell onions cooking and hear hamburgers sizzling as they fried. She watched a lady twirling candyfloss onto wooden sticks. 'It looks just like bright pink cotton wool,' she thought.

They watched the dodgem cars speeding round the rink and banging into each other. It looked fun.

'Would you like a go?' Daddy asked Katie.

'Yes, please,' she said. 'Can I drive?'

'If you like,' said Daddy, and strapped her

tightly into the driving seat.

But Katie was not quite big enough to steer the car on her own and everybody kept banging into them. She did not like that.

'I think I'd better help you,' said Daddy. He put his arm round her shoulder and a hand on the steering wheel. 'Now we'll show them!' he said, as they wove in and out of the other cars as fast as they could. Katie liked the dodgems.

They passed the stall where children were hooking plastic ducks.

'Can I have a go, please?' asked Katie. She gave the man her money and tried to hook one of the ducks onto her fishing rod. It was not as easy as it looked.

'Would you like me to help you?' said Mummy.

'No, thank you,' said Katie, 'I can do it myself.'

She kept on trying until she hooked a duck. It had a number 6 underneath. The man gave her a necklace as a prize. Katie put it round her neck proudly.

'Let's find a roundabout that Sarah can go on,' said Mummy, so they found one which had cars and buses on it. They put Sarah safely inside a bus, but Katie wanted to ride a big motorbike on the other side of the roundabout.

'All right,' said Daddy, 'but when the roundabout stops you must walk round here to find us.'

Katie agreed. Every time the motorbike passed Mummy and Daddy, they waved and she pooped the horn. The roundabout began to slow down, and Katie saw a balloon seller holding an enormous bunch of silver balloons. They were big and shiny and had cartoon characters on the side.

'I'd really like one of those,' thought Katie, 'I'll find out how much they cost.'

When the roundabout stopped, she jumped off and ran to look at the balloons. Then she turned round to run back to the roundabout where Mummy, Daddy and Sarah were waiting. But there were lots of roundabouts and Katie did not know which one to go to. She could not see the motorbike or the bus. She saw a man wearing a grey anorak. 'There's Daddy,' she thought, 'I'm all right now.' But the man was not Daddy. She saw a lady wearing a red coat. 'There's Mummy,' she thought, 'I'm all right now.' But the lady was not Mummy. She tried to shout but the music was too loud for anyone to hear. She was lost and she needed someone to help her. Katie looked at the people walking past. Perhaps there would be someone she knew and she could ask them to help her. But they were all strangers. Katie began to cry.

'Please God,' she prayed, 'I'm lost and I'm frightened. I can't find my mummy and daddy. Can *you* help me?'

She stood on tiptoe and tried to see over the top of the hoopla stall. She could not see Mummy, Daddy or Sarah.

A lady in a policewoman's uniform stopped to talk to her.

'What's the matter?' she said, 'Are you lost?' Katie nodded.

'I think I can help you,' said the lady, and she

talked to someone on her radio. 'Yes, that's right,' she said, 'little girl called Katie, five years old, blue duffle coat, black wellingtons, a scarf and a hat with a yellow pompom on top. Fine. I'll meet them at the Helter Skelter.'

She took Katie's hand. 'Come on,' she said, 'we've found your mummy and daddy. They're waiting at the Helter Skelter.'

'What's that?' asked Katie.

'It's like a big slide that goes round and round,' said the policewoman. 'You climb to the top and then sit on a mat and slide to the bottom. It's great fun.'

Katie saw her mummy and ran up to her. 'Are you going to tell me what happened?' asked Mummy. 'We were very worried about you.' Katie just cuddled her. She did not feel like talking just yet. Daddy said 'thank you' to the policewoman for helping Katie.

'Would you like a ride on the Helter Skelter before we go?' asked Mummy. 'I'll come too.'

Katie nodded. 'Yes, please,' she said quietly.

When they reached the bottom of the slide, Katie was laughing again. She looked up. Daddy was holding two big silver balloons. 'There's one for you and one for Sarah,' he said. 'I thought you might like one. Hold it very tightly or it will float up into the sky.'

'Thank you,' said Katie, 'I wanted one of those.'

On the way home, Sarah slept on Mummy's knee. In her hand she clutched a rather sticky lollipop.

Katie snuggled up to Daddy and gave a very big yawn.

'I'm pleased God sent the police lady to help me when I was lost,' she said, and she fell fast asleep, still clutching her big heart-shaped silver balloon.

Just a minute

Stephen was just biting into a crunchy green apple when suddenly . . . it happened! He ran as fast as he could into the kitchen to find his mum.

'Mum,' he shouted, 'where are you? I've got something really exciting to tell you.'

Mum was in the hall, talking to someone on the telephone. 'Just a minute,' she said, 'then you can tell me all about it, but I'm busy talking at the moment.'

Stephen waited . . . and waited . . . and waited.

Mum talked . . . and talked . . . and listened . . . and talked.

'A minute is a very long time,' thought Stephen, and he went to find his dad.

'Dad,' he shouted, 'where are you? I've got something really exciting to tell you.'

Dad was in the garage, mending the car. Stephen could just see his feet peeping out from underneath it.

'Just a minute,' said Dad in a rather muffled voice, 'I can't hear you properly while I'm working on the car. Come back in a few minutes and then you can tell me. I've nearly finished.'

Stephen shrugged his shoulders and went to find his grandma. She was sitting in an armchair in the lounge. He knew where she was because he could hear the clickety-click of her knitting needles. She was making a new jumper for him. It was bright blue and had a picture of a train on the front.

'Gran,' he shouted, 'I've got something really exciting to tell you.'

He was just going to tell her all about it when Gran realised that she had dropped a stitch somewhere and the pattern had gone wrong. She was rather annoyed that she had made a mistake and the balls of coloured wool were beginning to get twisted and tangled.

'Oh dear,' she muttered as she counted the stitches, 'wherever have I gone wrong? Let me see now . . . two red, five black, two red, five blue . . . what's that you said, dear? Something exciting? Wait a minute while I get this knitting sorted out, then you can tell me all about it,' and Gran carried on counting, 'Three red, two black, three red, two blue. . . .'

Stephen thought Gran was too busy to listen to him, so he went to find his big sister. Rachel was listening to a tape on her stereo. He tugged at her sleeve to let her know that he wanted to talk to her.

'Rachel,' he said, 'I've got something really exciting to tell you.' She moved the headphones away from one ear.

'This is my favourite tape,' she said, 'and I want

to listen to it. You can talk to me when this has finished, but I can't listen to you at the same time. Sorry.'

She carried on listening to the tape and tapping her feet in time to the music. Stephen walked away sadly. He was so excited but no-one wanted to listen. They were all too busy. Mum was still talking on the telephone, Gran was still trying to find out where her knitting had gone wrong, and he knew Dad must still be working on the car because he could hear the engine spluttering noisily.

Stephen went slowly upstairs to his bedroom and found his favourite teddy bear.

'Teddy,' he said, giving him a big hug, 'I've got something really exciting to tell you.' But Teddy just stared back, and when Stephen squeezed him the bear gave a very grumpy growl.

'Don't *you* want to listen to me today either?' he said, and put Teddy back on the bed. He thought for a moment. Suddenly he had an idea. 'I know,' he said, 'There is one person who is never too busy to listen to me,' and he sat on the bed and talked to God.

'My tooth's wobbly,' he said. 'This one at the top. I'm really excited because my friend says you get 10p when your tooth falls out.'

Stephen touched his wobbly tooth with his tongue and it wobbled even more. He touched his tooth with his fingers and wiggled it gently. He wobbled it and wiggled it and suddenly . . . it fell out!

19

'Mum,' he shouted at the top of his voice, 'look what's happened.' He ran out of the bedroom and went downstairs as fast as he dared. 'Look!' he said, 'My tooth's come out.'

'Why didn't you tell me it was loose?' she asked.

'I couldn't. You were too busy talking,' he answered.

Gran appeared. Stephen showed her his tooth.

'Well, fancy that!' she exclaimed. 'I didn't know it was loose.'

'I was going to tell you,' Stephen said, 'but you were too busy knitting.'

He showed it to Rachel.

'Why didn't you tell me it was wobbly?' she asked.

'You wouldn't let me,' he said, 'you were too busy listening to your tape.'

Dad appeared in the doorway. 'I suppose,' he said, 'that you didn't tell me because I was too busy working on the car?'

'Yes,' answered Stephen, 'and even Teddy wasn't interested. Nobody wanted to know about my wobbly tooth but I told God about it. My teacher at Sunday School said that God's never too busy to listen to you. You can talk to him about anything.'

'Quite right,' said Dad.

Stephen looked up at him slowly and gave him a cheeky grin.

'My friend says that if your tooth falls out and you put it under your pillow, then next morning the tooth has disappeared and you find some money there instead. Is that right too?'

Dad looked across at Mum. Then he smiled at Stephen.

'I think,' he said, 'you will have to try it and see!'

Cleopatra, the snooty camel

'What have we got here?' asked the lions curiously.

'We don't know,' said the elephants, trying to peer over the wall, 'but it looks rather like another camel.'

'Leave it to me,' said George the giraffe. He only had to stretch his long neck and he could see anything that was happening in the zoo.

The newest arrival at Twyford Zoo walked proudly into the camel house, her head held high.

'Hello,' said George, trying to be friendly as well as nosey, 'what's your name?'

'I'm Cleopatra,' drawled the camel lazily. She half opened one eye to look at him.

'That's a bit of a mouthful,' said George, 'do you mind if I call you Cleo for short? It's much easier to remember.'

'I most certainly *do* mind,' said the camel, 'my proper name is Cleopatra – she was a famous queen of Egypt, you know.'

'Really?' said George, who had never heard of her.

'Oh, yes,' said Cleopatra, 'I thought *everyone*

knew that.'

'My name's George,' said the giraffe, still trying very hard to be friendly.

'Oh, really?' said Cleopatra, 'George is such a plain name, I always think. Why don't you change it to something that sounds more important, like Horatio or Charlemagne? Or even Charles?' she added.

'Because I don't want to,' said George firmly. 'I *like* my name. Anyway, six Kings of England were all called George.'

'Oh, really?' said Cleopatra, who was not at all interested in anything anybody else told her.

George decided that he was wasting his time talking to a camel who thought that she knew everything, and everybody else knew nothing.

'What's she like?' asked the elephants, 'One hump or two?'

'One,' replied George, 'She's a snooty camel who thinks that she is the most important animal there is.'

'What's her name?' asked the lions.

'Cleopatra,' replied George.

'Cleo – what?' asked the lions.

'Cleopatra,' repeated George slowly, trying to mimic the way the camel spoke. 'She's named after a famous queen of Egypt, you know.'

'Really?' said the lions. They did not think that they wanted to be friends with a snobbish camel like Cleopatra.

The zoo-keepers came to bring fresh straw and fruit for the camels. Cleopatra immediately pushed past all the other camels and took the best pieces of fruit.

'I must have my vitamins, you know,' she told them. 'Do you know, when I was in Arabia, I won a competition for the best-looking camel? Only the best will do for me. I must keep my golden coat in perfect condition.'

The other camels looked at each other. Something would definitely have to be done about Cleopatra. They did not want to be friends with a greedy camel like her.

Cleopatra went for a walk around the enclosure and slowly chewed some grass. A kangaroo hopped across to talk to her.

'Hello,' said the kangaroo, 'where have you come from?'

'Arabia,' said Cleopatra. 'It's a beautiful place, you know. There is such a lot of sand and sunshine there and so many interesting things to see.'

'*I* come from Australia,' said the kangaroo, shyly.

'Oh, really?' said Cleopatra, fluttering her long eyelashes, 'I've never wanted to visit Australia.'

The kangaroo hopped away sadly. All Cleopatra wanted to do was talk about herself. The kangaroo did not want a friend like that.

Some donkeys were giving children rides on their backs. Cleopatra watched.

'When I was in Arabia,' she said to the llamas who lived on the other side of the fence, 'I gave a Sultan a ride across the desert. Sultans are very important people, you know.'

'Really?' said the llamas and carried on chewing grass. They wished that Cleopatra would stop talking about Arabia. They did not want a boring camel as their friend.

Soon all the animals had stopped talking to Cleopatra. Nobody wanted her to be their friend.

One day as she knelt in the camel house, feeling very lonely and sorry for herself, a cheeky sparrow flew in.

'What's the matter with you?' he asked. 'You shouldn't be inside on a beautiful day like this. The sun's shining and there are lots of children at the zoo today. Go on, go outside and give them a smile.'

A big tear rolled down the camel's cheek. 'I'm lonely,' she said, 'because nobody wants to be my friend. Nobody talks to me any more.'

'Well, if you ask me,' said the sparrow, cocking his head on one side, 'it's all your own fault. From what I've heard as I've been flying around this zoo, I'm not surprised that you haven't got any friends. I wouldn't want to have a snobbish, greedy, boring camel like you as a friend. I'm only talking to you now because I feel sorry for you.'

Cleopatra looked at the sparrow. 'That's *not* very kind,' she said.

'When you first came here,' said the sparrow, 'all the animals were kind to you and you were horrible to them. If you want to have friends you will have to be a lot kinder to the other animals in the zoo.'

'How do I do that?' asked Cleopatra.

'Simple,' replied the sparrow, 'First of all you think how you would like them to be kind to you, and then you treat them the same way. Smile at them and they'll smile at you. Share the best fruit and comfortable straw with the other camels, and for goodness sake, stop boasting about Arabia. Other places are just as interesting. Rajah the elephant could tell you some very interesting stories about India, or ask the lions to talk to you some time about Africa.'

Cleopatra stood up and slowly started to walk outside. The cheeky sparrow perched himself on her back. He had always wanted to ride on a camel.

'Look who's coming,' said the elephants.

'It's Cleo . . . er . . . Cleo whats-her-name,' said the lioness.

Cleopatra smiled, and this time it was a warm friendly smile.

'It's all right,' she said, 'you can just call me Cleo. All my friends do.'

'Oh, Thomas!'

Edward had a little brother. His name was Thomas.

When Thomas was a baby, he had big blue eyes and rosy cheeks. Whenever Nanna came to visit them, she would pick Thomas up and bounce him on her knee.

'Oh, Thomas,' she used to say, 'aren't you a beautiful baby?' and Thomas would chuckle and gurgle and dribble down his chin as if he understood exactly what she was saying.

When Thomas got bigger, he began to crawl.

He crawled into the kitchen and started to eat the cat's dinner. He crawled into the garden and ate soil. He crawled into the lounge and pulled all the reels of cotton out of Mum's workbox.

'Oh, Thomas,' laughed Mum, 'you're a little rascal, aren't you?' and Thomas would look at her with wide blue eyes, smile sweetly and blow her a very wet kiss.

Soon Thomas was big enough to walk. He walked into the kitchen and emptied a box of soap powder all over the floor. He walked into the lounge and drew on the wallpaper with Edward's wax crayons. He walked out into the garden, and then came in again and left muddy footmarks all over the kitchen floor, which Mum had just washed.

'Oh, Thomas,' said Mum crossly, 'you're a very naughty boy,' and Thomas looked at her with his big blue eyes and smiled, and Mum could not be cross for very long.

Then Thomas began to climb. When Mum put him into his cot at night, he climbed out. When she put him into his playpen, he climbed out. On Saturday mornings, Dad liked to stay in bed later, because he did not have to get up and go to work. But every Saturday morning, at five o'clock, Thomas climbed out of his cot and ran into Mum and Dad's room. Then he bounced on top of Dad until he woke up.

'Want to play,' said Thomas. 'Play with me, Daddy?'

'Oh, Thomas,' moaned Dad, with his eyes still half-closed, 'it's only five o'clock. Don't you *ever* sleep?' And Thomas would smile sweetly and tunnel under the bedclothes on Mum and Dad's bed. Thomas did not like sleeping.

One day, a lady came to talk to Mum. Mum made some tea and they sat down in the lounge. Edward and Thomas went to play in the garden. But Thomas crept back in again and climbed onto a chair next to where the lady was sitting.

'Look what *I've* got,' he said, and waved a fat, juicy worm in front of her eyes.

'Aarrgh,' screamed the lady, who did not like worms, and she spilled what was left of the tea on her skirt.

'I think I'd better be going,' she said, and hurried out of the door before Thomas showed her the worm again.

'Oh, Thomas,' said Mum, who did not know whether to laugh or be cross with him, 'whatever shall we do with you?'

One Saturday morning, Dad woke up at eight o'clock. 'Where's Thomas?' he said. 'He's usually running around before now.'

'Must be tired,' muttered Mum and turned over.

Edward came in. 'I think Thomas is ill,' he said. 'He's just lying there with his eyes shut. Come and see.'

Dad jumped out of bed. If Thomas was still lying in bed with his eyes shut at eight o'clock on a Saturday morning, there was definitely something wrong.

'I think we'd better send for the doctor,' he said.

The doctor thought that it would be better if Thomas went into hospital until they could find out what was the matter with him, and Mum went too in case he needed her.

Next day, Dad and Edward went to see Thomas and Mum went to talk to the nurse. Thomas lay in bed with his eyes closed.

'Oh, Thomas,' said Edward, 'please get better. It's really quiet at home without you.'

Thomas said nothing.

'Dad,' said Edward, 'we had a story at Sunday

School about Jesus. He made a little girl better when she was very ill. Jesus could make Thomas better too, couldn't he?'

'Yes,' said Dad.

'All right then, I'll ask him,' said Edward. 'Please Jesus,' he prayed, 'I want you to make my brother better.'

He opened his eyes and looked at Thomas. Thomas still lay there with his eyes closed.

'It hasn't worked,' Edward said, 'has it?' He was trying hard not to cry.

Dad sat him on his knee. 'Listen,' he said, 'when we talk to Jesus he always listens to what we say, but sometimes we have to wait for the answers.'

'Oh,' said Edward, 'but I wanted Thomas to get better *now*.'

'I know,' said Dad.

Edward gave Thomas a kiss. 'Bye,' he said, 'see you tomorrow,' and they went to talk to Mum.

The next day, Edward and Dad went to see Thomas. Thomas was sitting up in bed and the nurse was trying to give him some medicine.

'This is lovely, Thomas,' she said. 'Here you are.'

Thomas spat it out, all over the clean white sheets.

'Don't like it,' he told her, and climbed out of bed to meet Edward and Dad.

'Oh, Thomas,' said the nurse, 'you're supposed to stay in bed.'

'Don't want to,' said Thomas, and toddled down the ward to find some different toys to play with.

The nurse went after him and put him back in bed.

'Oh, Thomas,' she said, 'whatever shall we do with you?'

Edward looked at Dad. 'It worked, didn't it?' he said. 'Jesus *did* listen when I talked to him.'

'Yes,' smiled Dad, 'I think our Thomas is feeling much better!'

Have you seen the wind?

One night when it was dark and everybody was tucked up in bed, a strong wind began to blow. It whistled down the chimneys. It rattled letterboxes. It howled through the trees.

In a little cottage, an old man and an old woman were trying to sleep. The wind blew and blew. The chimney pots rattled, rain beat against the windows and the dustbin lid clattered as it blew off and rolled down the garden path.

'That wind's a nuisance tonight,' grumbled the old man, 'I can't sleep.'

'Neither can I,' complained the old woman, 'it's too noisy.'

Downstairs the tabby cat was curled up in her basket by the fire. She heard the rattling and the clattering and the whistling and the banging.

'It's too bad,' she hissed, 'how is a cat supposed to snooze on a night like this?'

Next morning the old man and the old woman were very, very grumpy.

'That wind kept me awake all night,' moaned the old woman.

'I wonder what damage it has done,' said the old man and went outside to look.

The dustbin had blown over. Paper was scattered all over the garden, flowers were lying broken on the ground. The old man and the old woman began to clear up all the mess. They muttered and moaned, moaned and muttered, and neither of them remembered to give the cat her breakfast.

The cat was hungry. 'I know,' she hissed, 'I'll go and find the wind and complain about all the trouble it has caused.'

She jumped over the garden wall and into the lane. 'Now,' she said, 'where do I start to look?'

She saw the ripples on the puddles. 'The wind is doing that,' she thought and kept walking past the puddles until she came to another cottage. The lady who lived there had hung out her washing on the line to dry. A big brown dog ran to the gate barking loudly.

'What do you want?' he growled.

'Have you seen the wind?' asked the cat.

'No,' he barked, 'but I suppose I could come and help you to look for it. Can you see those trees over there, bending and swaying? Look at all the leaves blowing off. That's where the wind must be.'

The tabby cat and the big brown dog marched down the lane until they reached the trees. The dog was right. There was a carpet of leaves on the ground, brown, orange and yellow, and lots more were still falling. A squirrel was scurrying around looking for nuts for her winter store. 'Have you seen the wind?' they asked.

'No, I haven't,' she said, 'but I suppose I could come and help you look for it. Look over there on the hill. Some children are flying kites. That's where the wind must be.'

So the cat and the dog and the squirrel went on down the lane towards the hill. On the way they passed a church with a tall steeple. A tiny grey mouse was scampering along the gate. 'Have you seen the wind?' they asked.

'No,' she answered, 'but I suppose I could come and help you look for it. I think you're going in the right direction because the golden cockerel on the weathervane is pointing towards the hill.'

So the cat and the dog and the squirrel and the mouse kept walking up the hill. Some sheep were grazing nearby.

'Have any of you seen the wind?' they asked.

'No,' bleated the sheep, 'but higher up the hill it's very cold and windy. Try up there.' One of the sheep said that she would go with them.

So the cat and the dog and the squirrel and the mouse and the sheep climbed to the very top of the hill. Down in the valley they could see a lake with lots of boats on it. They were moving very quickly and there were big ripples on the water.

'Look how the sails are billowing,' said the sheep. 'That's where the wind must be, down there.'

So they all ran down the hill as quickly as they could until they came to the lake.

'Hello,' they said to one of the ducks swimming

at the water's edge, 'have you seen the wind?'

'I'm afraid not,' she quacked, 'but I suppose I could come and help you look for it. There's a field over there with a scarecrow in it. His hat's just blown off. I think the wind is over there.'

So the cat and the dog and the squirrel and the mouse and the sheep and the duck went into the field. A few bright red poppies were swaying from side to side on their fragile stems, and some harvest mice were scampering about at the edge of the field collecting the ears of corn which the harvester had missed. The scarecrow stood all alone in the middle of the field and his hat had blown onto the top of the hawthorn hedge.

'Have you seen the wind?' asked all the animals.

'No,' squeaked the harvest mice, 'but in that wood over there there is an old oak tree. The wise old owl lives there and he is supposed to know everything. Would you like us to show you?'

'Yes, please,' they replied wearily. They had walked a long way.

So the cat and the dog and the squirrel and the church mouse and the sheep and the duck followed the harvest mice into the middle of the wood. High up in a gnarled old oak tree perched the wise owl.

'Twit-too-woo,' he hooted, 'what do you want? You're disturbing my sleep.'

'Please,' said the animals, 'have you seen the wind? We've looked everywhere. We saw it making ripples on the puddles in the lane, blowing washing dry, making trees sway, blowing leaves off them onto the ground, tossing kites into the air, making the sails on the boats billow. It even blew the scarecrow's old hat onto the hedge.'

'. . . and,' said the tabby cat, 'don't forget all the noise it made in the night.'

The old owl listened patiently.

'Listen,' he said, 'no-one has ever seen the wind. You can hear the noise it makes, you can feel it blowing all around you, but you will never see it.

'You can enjoy flying kites and sailing in boats when it's windy, you can be pleased when it dries the washing. You can see what it does but you will never find it. You have all been following the wind, trying to find out where it is blowing to but even I don't know where the wind is blowing to or blowing from. Only God knows that. There are some things that only he understands.'

The animals sighed. They were all very tired, especially the tabby cat who had walked the furthest. They thanked the wise old owl and started to walk slowly home.

The tabby cat reached the cottage and curled up in her basket by the warm fire.

'Where have you been?' asked the old man and the old woman, giving her a saucer of creamy milk.

She lapped it up, purred and fell fast asleep. She was just too tired to tell them.

We like chocolate cakes

It was a hot summer's day. The sun was shining brightly and because it was holiday time there was no playgroup or school to go to. Michelle and her friend Emma were playing happily in the Wendy house which Michelle's Mummy had put outside on the lawn. Her older brother, John, and his friend, Paul, had got some garden canes and old sheets and were trying to make a tent in the garden. Mummy was baking cakes. Soon a delicious smell came wafting from the kitchen. It made the children feel very hungry.

Michelle went to the kitchen door and saw a big tray full of chocolate cakes.

'Please could I have a cake,' she asked, 'and one for Emma as well?'

'No,' said her mummy, 'you can't have a cake but you can have a plain biscuit each if you like.'

'No, thank you,' said Michelle, 'we wanted chocolate cakes.'

She went back to the Wendy house.

'Mummy won't let us have any,' she told Emma, 'but don't worry – I've got an idea.' She looked in the box of dressing-up clothes. She found a pair of black high-heeled shoes, a blue dress, a pearl necklace and a hat with a big brim. Then she put on some red lipstick, picked up a big black handbag and walked back to the house. She had to walk very slowly because the shoes were too big and the heels were rather high. She knocked on the door and waited until her mummy came to see who was there.

'Good morning,' she said politely and speaking in a very posh voice, 'I'm a very important lady and I've come to visit you. My name is Mrs Smith.'

'Good morning Mrs Smith,' said Michelle's mummy, 'I'm very pleased to meet you. Do come in. I'm Mrs Davis.'

'What lovely chocolate cakes,' said the lady. 'Do you think I could have a cup of tea and two cakes please? I'm very hungry,' she added.

'I'm sorry,' said Mrs Davis, 'but I can't let you have any of the cakes. Would you like some plain biscuits instead?'

'No, thank you,' said the important lady, 'I'm going now. Goodbye.'

Michelle went back to the Wendy house. 'It didn't work,' she said. John came across the garden and she told him that Mummy would not let her have any chocolate cakes.

'Leave it to me,' he said. He looked in the box and found a policeman's helmet, a navy blue jacket and a black plastic moustache that had come out of a Christmas cracker.

'Mummy won't know who I am now,' he said.

He went to the kitchen door and knocked loudly.

'Good morning, madam,' he said in a very deep voice. 'I'm PC Edwards. I've come to check if there are any burglars in your house.'

'Well, I haven't seen any,' said his mummy, 'but you can come inside and look if you like.'

'That's very kind of you, madam,' said the policeman. 'Of course what I'd really like is a cup of tea and four of those delicious chocolate cakes. I'm very, very hungry.'

'I'm sorry,' said Mrs Davis, 'but I can't give you any of the cakes. Would you like some plain biscuits instead?'

'No, thank you,' answered John, 'policemen don't like plain biscuits very much. I'd better go now. Goodbye.'

He went back to the Wendy house. 'I didn't get any cakes either,' he said, 'but I've got an even better idea.' There were two old white sheets in the box. He gave one to Michelle. 'Put this over your head,' he said to her, 'and follow me. This is what we'll do.' He whispered something in her ear and she giggled.

He tapped lightly on the kitchen window. Then he and Michelle flapped their arms up and down.

'Whooo,' they said, 'whoooo.'

Their mummy came to the window. 'Goodness me,' she said, 'ghosts! In the daytime too! Whatever next?'

'Whoooo,' went the ghosts in a very eerie voice, 'we have come to scare you. But if you give us some of your lovely cakes we promise to go away.

Whooooooo!'

'I'm not frightened of ghosts,' said Mrs Davis, 'and I can't give you any cakes. Would you like some plain biscuits instead?'

'But we don't like those,' moaned the ghosts. 'Ghosts only like chocolate cakes.'

Just then the telephone rang and Mrs David went to answer it.

'Quick,' said John, 'there are lots of cakes here. Mummy won't miss four of them. You take two and I'll take two. Hide them under your sheet.'

They hurried back to the Wendy house and shared the cakes with Paul and Emma. Then they screwed up the paper cases and put them quickly into the dustbin.

Mummy came outside. She was very angry. 'Four of my cakes have gone,' she said. 'Who has taken them?' John and Michelle looked at the floor. There was silence.

'Perhaps it was that important lady,' said Michelle at last.

'Or the policeman,' said John.

'It might have been the ghosts,' said Michelle.

'Or it could have been you two,' said Mummy, 'couldn't it? Look at those crumbs on the rug you're sitting on.'

'How did you know it was us?' asked John.

'Lots of ways,' said Mummy. 'You see I know you two very well. The only small lady I know who wears shoes that are too big for her, and sucks her thumb at the same time, is Michelle. I don't know any real policemen who wear red trainers

like John's with their uniform, nor have I heard of
ghosts who like chocolate cakes, but I know that
they're your favourite kind of cakes.'

'Sorry,' they said.

'They were lovely cakes, Mrs Davis,' said Emma
quietly and trying very hard to be polite.

'Yes, I know they were,' Mrs Davis answered,
'but you see we were all going on a surprise picnic
after lunch – your family, Paul's family and us.
Now there won't be enough cakes for all of us
because there's no time to make any more.'

John looked at Michelle and groaned. 'I suppose
we'll have to take the plain biscuits?' he said.

'Yes,' said Mummy, 'we will.'

She put her arm around John's shoulder.
'Listen,' she said, 'we all do wrong things sometimes, even grown-ups do, and that makes God
very sad, but he still keeps on loving us. I didn't
like you taking my cakes, but I still love you.
You've both said "sorry" so now we'll forget about
it. Come on, hurry up and pack your things away.
It will soon be time for the picnic.'

I spy

Jamie and Richard were twins. They both had tousled ginger hair, lots of freckles, and mischievous grins. They looked so alike that their mum and dad were the only ones who could tell which twin was which, and even they got mixed up sometimes.

Mum bought them different coloured jumpers and socks so that other people would find it easier to tell the difference, but sometimes, because they were so mischievous, Richard would wear Jamie's blue jumper and blue socks, and Jamie would wear Richard's green jumper and green socks, and everyone got completely muddled up. And, because they were identical twins, they sometimes thought the same thing at the same time.

So, when Auntie Jenny came to take them out for the afternoon and asked them what they would like to do, no-one was surprised when Jamie said, 'let's go to the park near your house,' and Richard said, 'That's just what I was thinking.'

When they reached the corner of the road Auntie Jenny said, 'The bus is coming. Can you hurry up, or we'll miss it?'

'Of course,' said the twins at the same time.

'Race you to the bus stop,' said Jamie to Richard (or was it Richard to Jamie?) and they ran as fast as they could, with Auntie Jenny running behind them. The people in the bus queue smiled as they arrived, just in time to catch the bus.

'Can we go upstairs?' asked Jamie.

'Just what I was thinking,' said Richard, as he waited for their tickets to pop out of the ticket machine. 'Mum *never* lets us go upstairs on the bus, does she?'

'That's probably because it's not easy for her to carry a baby and a shopping bag upstairs while the bus is moving,' explained Auntie Jenny. 'It's easier for me – I've only got you two to look after.'

As the bus drove along the High Street, they saw all the people working in the offices above the shops. At one bus stop they could see ladies having their hair done at the hairdressers across the road. The people walking along the pavement looked much smaller, and the pigeons on the rooftops looked much bigger than usual.

'Look at the patterns in the brickwork around that window,' said Auntie Jenny, 'and those twisted brick chimneys.'

'You can see lots of interesting things from the top of a bus, can't you?' said Jamie.

'Just what I was thinking,' said Richard.

'Let's play "I spy",' suggested Jamie as they walked to the park. 'I spy with my little eye something yellow.'

'The sun,' guessed Auntie Jenny.

'The roses in that garden,' guessed Richard.

'No,' said Jamie.

A man was up a telegraph pole mending the wires.

'I know,' said Richard, 'it's the telephone van.'

'Yes,' said Jamie, 'your turn.'

'I spy something green,' said Richard.

'Leaves,' guessed Auntie Jenny,' or trees, or park gates or grass.'

'All wrong,' laughed Richard.

'Traffic lights,' suggested Jamie.

'Nearly right,' said Richard. 'You'll see it again in a minute.'

'Beep, beep, beep,' went the signal at the Pelican crossing.

'There's the green man,' said Auntie Jenny. 'It's safe to cross now.'

'Your turn,' said Richard. 'You've guessed what it was.' Auntie Jenny laughed.

'This one is quite hard,' she said. 'I spy something white. You'll have to look carefully.'

'The ice cream van,' shouted the twins as they heard the chimes.

'No,' said Auntie Jenny, 'guess again.'

'Those little daisies in the grass,' said Jamie.

'No.'

'The man sitting on that seat has got a white walking stick,' said Richard. 'Is it that?'

'Just what I was going to say,' said Jamie.

'So you're both right,' said Auntie Jenny. 'That's Mr Spencer and he's blind. He often comes for a walk in this park.'

'It must be very sad if you can't see,' said Jamie. 'You can't see all the different colours.'

'If he can't see anything, why does he come to the park?' asked Richard.

'Because he can still smell the roses and lavender in the flower beds and he can hear the birds singing. On a fine day he likes to sit on that seat over there, and feel the warm sunshine on his face. There are lots of things for him to enjoy in the park even if he can't see everything like you can.'

'Not quite the same though, is it?' said Jamie.

'No,' agreed Auntie Jenny, 'it isn't.'

They walked round the park and saw all the birds in the aviaries. They watched the peacock as it spread out its magnificent tail feathers into a fan.

'That's beautiful,' gasped the twins. 'Look at all those blues and greens.'

They walked round the lake and saw the ducks swimming along. Sometimes they dived down to find fish and only their tails showed above the water. 'The ducks look very funny when they do that,' said Richard.

Mr Spencer was still sitting on the park seat enjoying the sunshine. 'I think it's time we went home,' said Auntie Jenny, 'but I've forgotten to put my watch on. Perhaps Mr Spencer can tell us what the time is. I'll go and ask him.'

Jamie and Richard looked at her, very puzzled. 'But if he is blind,' they said, 'he can't see what time it is, can he?' Auntie Jenny went to talk to Mr Spencer and the twins followed. Mr Spencer

took out a watch from his waistcoat pocket and opened the top of it. Then he felt the little bumps on it with his fingers. 'It's nearly 4 o'clock,' he said, getting up from the seat. 'Time I was going home for my tea.'

'There's just time to eat an ice cream, before we catch the bus home,' Auntie Jenny told the twins, 'What kind would you like?' The twins were both walking along very slowly with their eyes shut, and their arms out in front of them. 'What are you doing?' she asked.

'Pretending to be blind,' they said. 'We're feeling our way along the path and smelling the flowers and listening to the birds.'

'In that case,' she said, '*I'll* choose the ice cream and you can find out what flavour it is by tasting it.' She gave them an ice cream each. 'Now, what flavour is it?' she asked.

'Mine's chocolate,' said Jamie.

'Mine's strawberry,' said Richard.

'Now open your eyes and see if your guesses are right,' said Auntie Jenny.

'I think it's fun pretending to be blind for just a little while,' said Jamie, 'but I'm glad that I can open my eyes and see lots of interesting things whenever I want to.'

'Do you know?' said Richard, 'that's just what I was thinking.'

He's coming!

'He's coming,' shouted Adam. 'I can see him coming up the road now!' He bounced up and down with excitement.

'Do you think that he'll have some more cards for us today?'

'I don't know,' answered Mummy, 'you will have to wait and see if he comes to our house, won't you? But if there are, you can help me to open them.'

Adam watched as the postman walked up and down the paths of the houses further down the road. He pressed his face up against the window so that he could see better, and watched as the window misted up where his warm breath touched the cold glass. Using his finger, he drew a picture of a house, and then suddenly remembered that Daddy got cross if he made marks on the windows, so he wiped it off again quickly.

He saw the postman go down the path of the house next door, he heard the rattle of the letterbox and the faint 'plop' as the letters landed on the doormat. Now it should be their turn. Adam felt very excited.

He heard the click of the catch on their gate and the sound of footsteps on the gravel path. Yes, he was coming at last. Adam rushed to the door and put his hands out ready to catch the letters as they came through the letterbox. But they did not come. Instead, the doorbell rang. Adam stood on tiptoe and tried to turn the doorknob. His mummy came to help him.

There stood the postman in his smart uniform, a heavy bagful of letters and cards on his shoulder. His cheeks were red and so was the end of his nose because it was very cold and frosty weather outside. He smiled at Adam.

'I've got a card and a parcel here for Master Adam Clark,' he said with a twinkle in his eye. 'Do you know him? I think he lives at this address.'

'Of course I do, that's me,' grinned Adam, 'I'm Adam Clark.'

'In that case,' said the postman, 'these must be for you.'

He gave Mrs Clark a bundle of cards and letters. He gave Adam a large envelope with a brightly coloured stamp on it, and a big oblong parcel wrapped in brown paper. 'Thank you,' said Adam and ran inside. He felt the parcel and shook it gently to see if it rattled. What could it be? A jigsaw? Some Lego? A game?

'Who is it from?' he asked.

'Uncle John, I think,' answered Mummy. 'He can't come and see us on Christmas Day because he has to go to work.' Uncle John was a doctor in a big hospital.

'Can I open it *now*?' he asked excitedly.

'No,' said his mummy, 'you have to save presents for Christmas Day.'

'Why? asked Adam, 'I want to open it now.'

'We open presents on Christmas Day,' said Mummy, 'because it reminds us of God's special present to us – baby Jesus. But, if you like, you can take off just the brown paper and put the parcel with all the others under the Christmas tree. Then you can come and help me to open all these cards and we can see who your card is from.'

Adam quickly tore off the brown wrapping paper and put his parcel under the tree. He still could not guess what was inside. He liked Christmas because it was so exciting. He liked opening the doors on his Advent Calendar and seeing what pictures were inside. There were only seven to open now. He liked the brightly coloured fairy lights, the shiny decorations and the glittering tinsel on the Christmas tree. He liked helping his mummy to make Christmas puddings and the cake, and making a wish as he stirred the mixture in the bowl. Best of all he liked opening cards and presents.

Mummy and Adam sat down in the lounge and began to look at what the postman had brought. There was a brown envelope addressed to Daddy.

'Oh dear,' said Mummy. 'That looks like the electricity bill. He won't like that!' and she put it on the shelf for Daddy to open later. The others were all cards. There were pictures of angels, shepherds, robins, Christmas trees, pictures of baby Jesus, all sorts of pictures.

'Why do people send cards at Christmas?' asked Adam.

'Well, usually to wish their friends and family a happy Christmas. People often send cards to friends they don't see very often to let them know that they still think about them. People send cards to remind each other about the Christmas story – how Jesus was born as a baby in a stable and the shepherds and wise men came to visit him.

Adam opened his card. It was from Stephen, the boy who used to live in the house next door to them. Adam and Stephen used to go to playgroup together until Stephen's family moved to a new house.

'There you are,' said Mummy, 'you see, Stephen hasn't forgotten you. It says, "Happy Christmas. Lots of love from Stephen". Isn't it lovely, and look at all those kisses he's written inside. Would you like to make a special card to send to him? I could help you when we get back from the shops.'

'Yes, please,' said Adam eagerly and ran to put on his coat and scarf.

When they went shopping, Mummy and Adam went to the newsagents. They bought some glue and a tube of silver glitter and a roll of red sellotape with a green holly pattern on it.

'We could make a card that looks like a parcel,' said Mummy.

'That's a good idea,' said Adam.

When they got home they put newspaper on the

kitchen table and Mummy found a piece of red paper which she folded in half. Then she helped Adam to put two pieces of sellotape across the front so that it looked like a parcel.

'It hasn't got a label on it,' said Adam. 'All parcels need a label.'

'All right,' said Mummy and cut a piece of white card into the right shape. 'What do you want to write on it?'

'To Stephen with love from Adam,' he told her, so Mummy wrote the words lightly in pencil and Adam wrote over the letters in red crayon. Then he squeezed some blobs of glue on the card and carefully sprinkled the glitter on top. It looked lovely.

Inside the card, Adam stuck a piece of brown paper to make a manger and drew a picture of the baby Jesus sleeping inside it. Then he fetched a few pieces of clean straw that they used for bedding for their rabbit and cut them into smaller pieces. He stuck those on his picture as well, and wrote lots of kisses inside the card.

'It's finished now,' he said. 'Do you like it?'

'I think it's beautiful,' Mummy told him.

'When Stephen opens it he'll remember about Jesus being God's special present to us, won't he?' said Adam.

'Yes,' said Mummy, 'he will.'

'Do you think Uncle John would like a card like that?' asked Adam. 'I could make another one the same.'

'I think,' said Mummy, 'that's a very good idea.'

Grandpa and the bird table

'Grandpa,' said Craig, 'could you help me to make a bird table please?' He climbed onto Grandpa's knee, put his arms round his neck and gave him a big smile. 'Please, Grandpa, could you?'

Grandpa looked at Craig. 'Well, that depends,' he said slowly, 'on what you want, why you want it, and whether I've got enough wood to make it.'

Craig told him all about the television programme they had watched at school. 'When it's cold weather,' he said, 'the birds will die if they don't get enough food and water, so I want to help them.'

'Oh, I see,' said Grandpa, 'so what sort of table do you want to make? Shall we try to draw it?'

He found an old envelope and a pencil. Then he thought for a minute. 'I think,' he said slowly, 'we ought to start with a square piece of wood and put four strips of wood along the sides to stop the bread falling off. Do you?' He drew some lines on the paper to show Craig what he meant.

'Yes,' agreed Craig, 'and we need to put the table on a post or something. If it's on the ground the cats will chase all the birds. We can dig a hole for the post to go in the ground.'

Grandpa looked out of the window. The roof-tops and the bare branches of the trees were coated with white powdery frost. 'No, Craig,' he said, 'it's cold and frosty. The ground will be far too hard to dig a hole. We'll have to put legs on the bottom of the post so that it will stand on the path. Now is that all?'

'Can it have a house on the top for the birds to shelter in?' asked Craig. 'The bird tables in the pet shop have got houses on top.'

'I don't think we'll have time to do all that today,' said Grandpa, 'but how about this instead?' He drew a piece of wood on one side of the table and another on the opposite side. 'Those are the walls,' he told him. 'Then we can put some more pieces of wood across the top to make a sloping roof so the birds will have a shelter.'

Grandpa pulled on his overalls that he wore whenever he was doing woodwork. He put a checked cap on his head to keep his bald patch warm and put his pencil behind his ear. Then he took Craig down the garden path to his shed.

Grandpa was very proud of his shed. All his tools were arranged neatly on hooks around the walls. There were saws, hammers, planes, screw-drivers, chisels – everything he needed to make things out of wood. On the shelves were jars and tins full of all kinds of screws and nails, and in one corner was a big box full of oddments of wood.

'Here we are,' said Grandpa, pulling out a square

piece of wood, 'this is just what we need for the table.' He gave Craig some sandpaper. 'You can use that to make the wood smooth,' he said, and showed him what to do.

Craig rubbed and rubbed until his arm ached. He watched Grandpa planing a big piece of wood for the post. He liked the way the curly woodshavings came out at the end.

'I want to do that,' he said, 'Please can I?'

'No,' said Grandpa, 'you're not quite old enough. You might damage the plane.'

He took a saw down from a hook and began to cut a long length of wood into pieces. 'Can I do that?' Craig asked, 'Please can I?'

'Not with this saw,' replied Grandpa, 'it's too big and sharp for you. I'll find you a smaller one, but be very careful so that you don't cut yourself.'

He stood behind Craig and helped him to saw the wood into four pieces. 'These need smoothing next,' he said. 'You can do that, can't you?'

'Yes,' said Craig, but he was tired of sanding wood. It made his arm ache. He wanted to do something more exciting. Grandpa went outside and Craig decided to look around the shed. He found the steel rule that Grandpa used for measuring. He pulled it out and then pressed the yellow button in the middle so that the ruler sprang back inside. That was fun, so he did it again. He reached for the big hammer and a tin of nails. 'I'll nail the pieces of wood onto the table,' he thought, 'I can do that myself.'

He hit the first nail with the hammer, and the

nail bent. He hit the second nail and that bent too. He tried again and he hit his thumb instead. 'Ouch!' he shouted, and knocked the tin of nails all over the floor.

Grandpa rushed in, 'Whatever are you doing?' he said crossly. 'If we're going to get this table finished today you will have to help me properly. Please pick those nails up.'

'Sorry,' muttered Craig as he crawled on the floor to find all the nails which he had dropped. Grandpa kept hammering and sawing and soon the table was nearly finished. 'There's just the roof to put on now,' he said, 'but this time, my lad, we'll use a smaller hammer and *I'll* show you how to knock the nails in.'

The bird table looked very good. 'It really needs some varnish on it,' said Grandpa, 'but your dad can do that later, when you take it home. We'll go to the shop and buy some peanuts, then we'll ask Granny for a big darning needle and some string to thread them onto. She might have some bacon rinds or fat we could hang up too. The blue tits like that.'

So that is what they did. They put some pieces of bread and a bowl of water on the table, and hung up the strips of peanuts and fat. Then they went inside and watched quietly for the birds to come and discover the food.

Soon there were big starlings, squabbling and fighting over the pieces of bread. There were thrushes with speckled breasts. Some blue tits balanced on the string as they pecked at the

peanuts; there were lots of sparrows, a blackbird with a bright yellow beak, and even a robin redbreast. He was Craig's favourite.

'You might see more kinds of birds when you put the table in your garden at home,' Grandpa told him, 'God has made lots of different kinds – big ones, little ones, pretty ones, and plain ones, and he cares about all of them. I think he'll be very happy that you are helping to care for them too.'

'But you helped as well,' said Craig, reaching up to give him a big kiss. 'Thank you, Grandpa.'

That's what a family is for

'Nicola was crying at Sunday School today,' said Lucy, as she and her family sat down to eat their lunch.

'So what?' said Richard, her big brother, 'Girls are always crying!'

'That's not fair,' said Lucy, 'Nicola was crying because she was sad.'

'Who's Nicola?' asked Mummy.

'She's got a red and blue dress with a white collar and she's got brown hair, tied in a pony tail.'

'Oh,' said Mummy, who still had no idea who Nicola was, 'what's her other name?'

'Ann, I think,' said Lucy.

'Her name's Nicola Jones,' muttered Richard, 'her brother Carl's in my class at school. They moved here a few weeks ago.'

Lucy was beginning to get impatient. 'Don't you want to know *why* she was so sad?' she asked.

'Of course we do,' said Daddy quietly. 'Why *was* Nicola sad?'

'Because her daddy is in hospital. He had an accident at work last week. He's very, very ill.

Nicola is frightened that he's doing to die.'

'Oh,' said Mummy, 'I see.'

'Mrs Jeffries said that we've all got to be extra kind to Nicola and look after her,' said Lucy, 'and we asked God to make her daddy better.'

'Where does Nicola live?' asked Daddy.

'I don't know,' said Lucy, 'but it's a big house and Nicola has to cross two busy roads to come to Sunday School. That's why Mrs Jeffries usually brings her in her car.'

'Perhaps I'd better ask Mrs Jeffries where Nicola lives,' said Daddy, 'then we can ask what we can do to help. Is that all right?'

'Yes, thank you,' said Lucy. As well as being her daddy, Mr Griffiths was also the vicar at their church.

So, on Monday, Mr Griffiths went to talk to Nicola and her mummy. Then he went to the hospital to visit her daddy.

On Tuesday morning, Mrs Wood came to help Lucy's mummy to do the housework. While Mrs Wood was dusting, Lucy told her about Nicola.

'Her daddy had an accident at work last week,' she said.

'Where was he working?' asked Mrs Wood.

'I don't know,' said Lucy, 'but it was at a factory with an enormous chimney. Nicola said he was mending the chimney and he fell.'

Mrs Wood looked across at Lucy's mummy. 'I read about that in the paper,' she said, 'fell from some scaffolding, he did. They say he's lucky to be alive. Such a shame, isn't it?' They only moved into that big house near the park a few weeks ago.'

'Mrs Jeffries said that we've got to look after Nicola,' said Lucy.

'Of course we have,' said Mrs Wood.

So, on Wednesday, Mrs Wood went to Nicola's house. She took some raspberries, some scones and a pot of home made jam. Mrs Jones was very pleased to see her. Mrs Wood looked out of the window at the garden. It had two lawns, and there was a tall hedge growing all around it. 'It's a lovely garden,' she said.

'Yes,' agreed Mrs Jones, 'but I haven't got much time to look after it at the moment.'

I'll have a word with my George, thought Mrs Wood. Mr Wood liked gardening and whenever the grass near the church needed cutting, Mr Wood got out his lawn mower and cut it. On Sundays, Mr Wood stood by the door and gave everybody a hymn book as they came into church.

So, on Thursday, Mr Wood went round to Nicola's house and he mowed the lawns and cut the hedge. Mrs Jones was very pleased. Nicola thought that Mr Wood looked different when he was not wearing his best suit.

On Thursday night, Miss Lucas came to talk to the vicar about the hymns they were going to sing at Family Service. Miss Lucas played the organ at their church. Lucy told her all about Nicola.

'Mrs Jeffries says that we've got to look after Nicola,' said Lucy.

'Of course we have,' said Miss Lucas, 'that's what a family is for, isn't it?'

'What did she mean?' Lucy asked her mummy later, 'I didn't understand.'

'Well,' said Mummy, 'a church isn't just a building, it's the people as well. We're like a family – God's family – and we have to look after each other.'

'Why?' asked Lucy.

'Because that's what God wants us to do,' said Mummy.

So on Friday night, on her way home from work, Miss Lucas took a big bunch of flowers to Nicola's house. Mrs Jones was very pleased to see her. She put some of the flowers in a vase. 'I'll take the rest to the hospital,' she said, 'to cheer my husband up.

On Saturday afternoon, Lucy and her family were going swimming at the Sports Centre.

'Could Nicola and her brother come with us?' asked Lucy.

'Yes, of course, if their mummy will let them,' said Daddy.

So when Mrs Jones went to the hospital, Nicola and Carl went to the vicarage.

'Does your daddy wear his white collar when he goes swimming?' whispered Nicola.

Lucy looked puzzled. 'No,' she said, 'just his blue swimming trunks.'

'Oh,' said Nicola. She had never seen the vicar without his special collar.

At the swimming pool, they zoomed down the water slide and laughed as the water splashed all over them. Nicola showed Lucy her ten metre

badge. 'We used to go to swimming lessons,' she told her.

'Dad taught me to dive,' Carl said quietly, 'he used to take us swimming every Saturday.'

'And when he's better he'll be able to take you again,' said Mr Griffiths. 'I like diving too. Are you going to come down to the deep end with me and jump off the diving boards?' So off they went.

'Your dad's good fun, isn't he?' said Carl, 'Can I come here with you again?'

'Of course,' said Richard.

When Mrs Jones came back from the hospital she was smiling. 'Dad's a lot better today,' she said, hugging Carl and Nicola. 'The doctors think that he will be able to walk again soon, but he won't be able to go to work for a long time.'

'I'm pleased your daddy is getting better,' said Lucy. 'Are you going to tell Mrs Jeffries tomorrow?'

'Of course I am,' said Nicola.

'Thank you for taking the children swimming,' said Mrs Jones, 'and thank you for everything you've done to help us.' She bent down and gave Lucy a kiss.

'Thank you, Lucy,' she said, 'for looking after Nicola.'

'That's all right,' said Lucy, 'Mummy said that's what a family is for.'

'See you tomorrow, Lucy,' said Nicola.

'Yes,' said Mrs Jones, 'we will.'

Big trouble and the blackbird

Cyril was a centipede – a very silly centipede. Whatever anybody told him to do, he did exactly the opposite. Now, if *your* mum told you to 'stand still' you would stand very still and not move, (well, wouldn't you?), especially if you were standing near a busy road? But if Cyril's mum told him to stand still, he always scuttled away as fast as he could.

And if *you* were told to 'hurry up' you would move as quickly as you could, but if Cyril was told to 'hurry up' . . . can you guess what happened? Of course, he crawled very, very, slowly.

'You must learn to do what you are told,' said his mum, 'or one day you will get into BIG TROUBLE.'

'What's trouble?' asked Cyril.

'It's when things go wrong, or you get into a mess and you don't know how to get out of it again,' explained Mum.

'Oh,' said Cyril, who had not really understood what she had said. Anyway, it might be rather exciting to find out what BIG TROUBLE was, especially as his mum had told him to keep away from it.

Cyril and his family lived in a hole under a large stone in the garden. It was dark there, and no-one could see them. A family of woodlice lived under the same stone, and they usually waited until night-time before they crawled out and started to look for something to eat.

One day, when the sun was shining brightly, Cyril decided to go for a walk. 'I'm hungry,' he thought, 'I'll go and find something to eat. A tiny insect or two would make a delicious snack.'

The woodlice woke up and looked at Cyril as he began to crawl out from underneath the stone.

'Come back,' they said, 'or you could get into BIG TROUBLE, Don't you know that it's dangerous for an insect like you to walk down a garden path on a sunny day?'

Cyril turned his head round very slowly. 'But I want to go for a walk *now*,' he said, 'I'm hungry.'

'*Please* come back,' said the woodlice. 'If you don't, the big blackbird might come along and pick you up in his big, yellow beak and then he'll E – A – T you.' They shivered because they were so frightened of the big blackbird. If they ever saw him, they curled up into tiny round balls and pretended that they were pebbles until he went away again.

'But Cyril can't do that,' said William Woodlouse to his sister, 'because he's a centipede not a woodlouse. His body is too long and he's got *far* too many legs.'

Cyril was not very good at spelling, and had no idea what word E – A – T spelt, so he was not afraid. He thought it would be exciting to go and find out all about the big blackbird and BIG TROUBLE. It *must* be good if his mum and the woodlice had both told him to keep away from it. So he went on, across the rockery and onto the garden path.

'What a lovely day,' he thought as he looked at all the brightly coloured flowers at the side of the path. Because he was such a small centipede, they looked as tall as trees.

Some ants were bustling about, collecting pieces of dead leaves to take back to their nest. They looked at Cyril as he crawled lazily past them (which took quite a long time because centipedes have long bodies with lots of segments and lots of pairs of legs – rather like a long railway train with lots of carriages and pairs of wheels).

'What are *you* doing here?' the ants asked. 'We don't often see a centipede going past our house.'

'I'm going for a walk,' replied Cyril, 'I'm hungry so I'm looking for food.'

'Oh,' said the ants, hoping very much that centipedes did not like ants for breakfast. 'Be careful, because the big blackbird is flying about looking for insects like you. Go home, or you could be in BIG TROUBLE. If he sees you he might E – A – T you.'

Cyril took no notice. It was far too nice a day to go home just yet. Besides, he still had not seen the big blackbird or found the BIG TROUBLE everyone was talking about, but he knew that they must be somewhere in the garden. He wondered why the blackbird was looking for insects like him.

Just then, a black shadow came over the path like a big, black, cloud.

'I'd better go home,' thought Cyril, 'I think it's going to rain.' He turned his long body completely round to face the opposite direction. The ants had suddenly disappeared and there on the path in front of him was what looked like an enormous bridge.

'That's funny,' he thought to himself, 'that bridge wasn't here a few minutes ago?'

He felt something touch his back. He looked up. It was a big, yellow beak and above it were two dark glistening eyes. The beak began to open and Cyril felt very frightened. It was the big blackbird. Suddenly he knew what BIG TROUBLE meant and it was easy to guess what word E – A – T spelt. If he did not hurry up and escape, the big blackbird would EAT him.

Whatever could he do? He was too big to go down the tiny hole at the opening to the ants nest, and he could not curl himself into a ball and pretend to be a pebble as he had seen the wood-lice do. Perhaps, if he hid his legs under his body and stayed very still, the bird would think he was a piece of twig? . . . He stretched himself out and something very strange happened. His skin split. Because Cyril was only a young centipede he did not know that when a centipede grows and his old skin becomes too small, it splits open leaving a

new skin underneath. Very carefully and slowly Cyril crept out and crawled as fast as all his legs would carry him back to the rockery and safety, leaving the blackbird to peck at the old skin he had left behind.

'Hurry up,' said his mum. And this time Cyril did exactly what he was told.

Something special for tea

Charlotte liked staying with Grandma and Grandpa. They lived in a little village which was very different from the big city where she usually lived. The shops were smaller and very different from the big supermarket where Charlotte and her family went to buy food. The streets in the village were narrow, not at all like the wide, busy roads near her home. Grandpa used to be a farmer but he had sold the farm and he and Grandma had gone to live in a little cottage nearby. It had a thatched roof and old-fashioned windows with small panes of glass in them. Best of all, there were three ponies in the field next to the cottage, and sometimes the people who owned them allowed Charlotte to go for a ride on the smallest one, which was chestnut and white and called Amber. Charlotte gave Amber pieces of carrot to munch as she stroked the pony's long silky mane. She felt very sad that it was almost the end of her holiday.

'Put your coat on,' said Grandma, 'and we'll go to the shops. Your mummy and daddy are coming this afternoon and I want to buy something special for tea.'

They walked down the lane, past the grey stone church with its pointed spire, and onto the street where the shops were. As they reached the bakery, Charlotte stopped and looked at all the different kinds of cakes in the windows. There were doughnuts, iced buns, gingerbread men, chocolate eclairs and strawberry jam tarts. Charlotte thought they all looked delicious. She hoped Grandma would buy some for tea.

'What are those?' she asked, pointing at a tray of currant buns with crosses on top, 'I haven't seen any like that before.'

'They're called hot cross buns,' said Grandma. 'They're a special sort of bun that you can only buy at Easter time.'

'Can we try some, please?' asked Charlotte.

'Perhaps,' replied Grandma, and went into the bakery to buy some bread. Charlotte watched as Grandma did her shopping, but she did not see her buy any buns. Charlotte felt very disappointed.

When they got back to the cottage, Grandma put the bread in the pantry and brought out some flour, sugar, margarine, salt, spices, dried fruit and candied peel. Then she took a clean apron out of the kitchen drawer and wrapped it round Charlotte.

'Now,' said Grandma, 'wash your hands.'

'What are we going to make?' asked Charlotte.

'Hot cross buns, of course,' replied Grandma, 'wasn't that what you said you wanted for tea today? You thought I'd forgotten, didn't you?'

Charlotte nodded. Then she smiled.

Grandma weighed some flour on the scales and tipped it into a mixing bowl. 'Now,' she said, 'we want a pinch of salt and some spices, and some margarine.' She rubbed the margarine into the flour until the mixture was crumbly, then she grated a little bit of lemon rind in as well to make the buns taste good. She gave Charlotte a big spoon. 'It's your turn next,' she told her, 'we need three big spoonfuls of dried fruit, one of candied peel, and one of sugar. Can you manage that?'

'Of course,' said Charlotte, and put them carefully into the bowl. 'Is that all?'

'No,' answered her grandma, 'we haven't put in the most important ingredient yet. Here you are. Crumble this into the basin.'

She gave Charlotte a small paper bag with yeast in it. The yeast was greyish brown, very crumbly, and smelled different from anything else Charlotte had ever smelled. She put a tiny crumb in her mouth to taste it. She thought it was horrible and pulled a face.

'Oh dear,' she thought, 'perhaps I won't like hot cross buns after all!'

Grandma realised what she was thinking. 'You need yeast to make the dough rise,' she explained, 'otherwise the buns will be flat and hard. Wait and see. The buns will be delicious when they are finished.'

Grandma added some warm milk and a little bit of sugar to the yeast in the basin. 'Watch it,' she said to Charlotte, 'and see what happens.'

Sure enough, the yeast mixture began to get bubbly and frothy, and then Grandma added it to the flour mixture in the big bowl and kneaded it until it was a smooth round ball. Then she covered the bowl with a damp cloth and left it on the kitchen table while she peeled the vegetables and made an apple pie for dinner. Charlotte went to do a jigsaw. When she came back into the kitchen she peeped at the dough in the bowl. She could hardly believe her eyes.

'Grandma,' she shouted excitedly, 'look at this. It's grown!'

Grandma looked. 'Yes,' she said, 'the yeast has made the dough rise.' She pushed her finger into the dough and the dough bounced back so that the hole she had made disappeared. Charlotte laughed.

'When I went to playgroup we had some pink Playdoh that did that,' she told her.

Grandma put the dough onto a floured board and pulled and punched it for a few minutes. Then she cut it into smaller pieces, and Charlotte helped her to knead them into bun shapes which they put onto a baking tray. Grandma gave Charlotte some pastry, left over from the apple pie. 'Roll these out,' she told her, 'and we'll cut some strips to make the crosses on top. You can't have hot cross buns without any crosses on top.'

'Why do you put crosses on top?' asked Charlotte.

'Well,' said Grandma, 'the crosses are to remind us of the Easter story. Tomorrow is Good Friday, which is a special day every year when people

remember how Jesus died on a cross. It wasn't really a good day but a very sad one because Jesus hadn't done anything wrong.'

'But that's not fair,' said Charlotte. 'Why did he have to die?'

'Because some people didn't like Jesus and the kind things he did, so they told the soldiers to take him away. His friends were very upset but, two days later, when Jesus came alive again, they were very, very happy.'

Grandma and Charlotte carefully put the buns in the hot oven and left them to cook. Soon they were golden brown. Grandma took them out of the oven and Charlotte brushed them with sugar and water to make the tops shiny. She could hardly wait to taste them.

When it was tea-time and Charlotte's mummy and daddy had arrived, they all sat down at the table. In the middle was a big plate full of buttered hot cross buns, and everyone agreed that they were the best buns they had ever tasted.

'We must remember to make some of these next Easter,' said Mummy, 'if Grandma gives us the recipe.'

'Yes, please,' said Charlotte, 'and I'll tell you all about putting crosses on the top of them.'

Our new baby

'What are *you* doing here?' asked Daniel sleepily.
He sat up in bed. 'And where,' he asked, 'is my
mummy?'

Grandma smiled. Grandma often smiled but this
was a really big, extra-special kind of smile.

'Last night,' she told him, 'when you were fast
asleep, Mummy went into hospital to have the
baby. Daddy drove her there in the car. So I've
come to look after you.'

'Oh,' said Daniel. His mummy had never gone
away from home before and left him behind.
Grandma was very nice, but Grandma was not
quite the same as his mummy, was she?'

He climbed out of bed, washed his face and
hands and went downstairs in his dressing-gown.
Grandma had put his breakfast on the table.

'Here you are, Daniel,' she said brightly. 'I've
made you a lovely bowl of porridge, a boiled egg
and some toast.'

Daniel looked at the porridge. He put his spoon
in it. It was just like Mummy Bear's porridge in
the Goldilocks story. It was too thick and lumpy.

'Grandma,' he said, 'you've made this porridge all wrong. My mummy doesn't make it like this. It's too thick.'

Grandma added some cold milk and swirled it into the porridge. 'Try that,' she said.

Daniel ate it. Then he looked at the squares of toast on the plate.

'Grandma,' he said, 'this toast is the wrong shape. My mummy doesn't make it like this. She cuts it into fingers, then I dip them in my egg.'

Grandma cut the toast into smaller pieces and took the top off his egg. 'Try that,' she said.

Daniel looked at his egg.

'Grandma,' he said, 'this egg is too hard. My mummy doesn't make it like that.'

'Well, I'm very sorry,' said Grandma, 'but I can't do anything about that.' Daniel wondered why she was not smiling any more. Just then, the door opened and Daddy came in. He flung his arms round Daniel and lifted him high into the air.

'Guess what, Daniel,' he said, 'you've got a baby sister. What do you think about that then?' Daniel was not sure. He really wanted a brother, but he thought you probably could not change babies once they had arrived. Anyway, Daddy seemed pleased.

'When can I see Mummy and the baby?' he asked.

'This afternoon, but only if you are a good boy,' he told him. 'I've got to go to work now, but I'm sure your grandma can't wait to see her new grand-daughter.' Grandma smiled.

When Daddy had gone to work, still smiling and whistling happily, Daniel put on his favourite sweatshirt and jeans. He thought about his new baby sister and wondered what she would look like. Grandma wanted to go to the wool-shop and buy some pink wool to make her a jacket.

'Can I buy her a present too?' asked Daniel.

'Of course,' said Grandma, 'what do you want to buy?'

'A football,' said Daniel.

'I think she's too small to play football,' said Grandma.

'I'll buy her a really big doll instead,' said Daniel.

'I think the big doll would be bigger than the baby,' Grandma told him, 'but I know a shop that sells lots of things for babies. I'll take you there and you can choose something. How about that?' Daniel agreed.

On the way there, they walked past a sweetshop.

'I know,' said Daniel, 'I'll buy her some sweets.'

'Tiny babies can't eat sweets,' said Grandma. 'They don't have any teeth, but we can buy some of Mummy's favourite sweets. You can give them to her when we go to the hospital.' Daniel thought that was a good idea.

Daniel did not know what to choose for the baby. There were clothes and rattles and building bricks and cuddly toys. He saw some small furry teddy bears and picked one up. It had a red satin bow tied tightly round its neck and, when he shook the teddy, a bell jingled inside it. Grandma helped

him to pay the lady at the cash desk.

'I've got a new baby sister,' he told the lady proudly. 'This is her present.' The lady said he was a very lucky boy.

When they got home, Grandma helped him to wrap his presents in pretty paper, and after lunch they went to the hospital. It was a big building with lots of long corridors and lots of floors, just like an enormous block of flats. Grandma had to keep asking people which way to go, but at last they opened some more doors and there was Mummy sitting in bed and holding the baby. Daniel stood still and looked. He wondered if Mummy could cuddle him and his sister at the same time.

'Come here, Daniel,' said Mummy, 'say hello to your new sister.'

He moved a little nearer. Mummy stretched out one arm. 'Come on,' she said, 'how can I give you a cuddle if you stand so far away?'

Daniel smiled and snuggled up to her. He looked at the baby. She had black skin just like his, and soft curly hair. He stroked her cheek gently with his fingertips. Mummy held his little finger. 'Hold it here,' she said, and, as it touched the baby's hand, she wrapped her tiny fingers tightly round it.

'I think she likes me,' he said, beaming proudly.

'Of course she does,' said Mummy, 'you're her big brother.'

He gave Mummy the presents. She liked her sweets and when she moved the teddy nearer the baby, his sister waved her tiny hands just a little bit so that he could see her pink palms.

'She likes the sound of the bell,' said Mummy.

'What's her name?' asked Daniel.

'How about Caroline?' said Mummy.

'Yes,' said Daniel, 'I like that.'

Soon they had to go home. Daniel was very quiet.

'What's the matter?' asked Grandma, holding his hand, 'don't you like your new sister?'

'Yes,' said Daniel, 'she's lovely, but I want my mummy. When is she coming home?'

'Soon,' said Grandma, 'but we can go to the hospital again tomorrow if you like.'

'Can she love me as well as the baby?' he asked her.

'Of course,' Grandma said, 'why ever not?'

'Just wondered,' he said.

'Daniel,' said Grandma, 'you will always be special to your mummy and daddy. I think you're special too because you're the only grandson I've got. But there's someone else who loves you and thinks you're special and that's God.'

'Oh,' said Daniel, 'does God love Caroline too?'

'Of course,' said Grandma, 'and Mummy and Daddy and me. Everyone is special to God.'

Daniel smiled. He felt very happy. He hopped and skipped all the way home and whenever he met anyone he knew he told them with a big smile, 'I've got a new baby sister. Her name's Caroline.'

Everyone said, 'Aren't you a lucky boy?' and Daniel answered, 'Yes, I am!'

Lost and found

'Happy Birthday,' said Dad. He kissed Mum and gave her a parcel. It was small, wrapped in pink tissue paper and tied with a pink and gold striped ribbon.

'That looks interesting,' she said, smiling as she untied the ribbon bow.

Inside the parcel was a box and, as Mum slowly lifted the lid, she saw a beautiful pair of gold earrings. They were shaped like flowers and had a red ruby in the centre of each one.

'They're lovely,' she exclaimed, 'they're the nicest pair of earrings I've ever had. Thank you,' and she gave Dad a big hug.

After that, whenever she was going anywhere special, or if she was wearing her best red dress, Mum always wore the earrings which Dad had given her for her birthday. The children called them her special earrings.

One day Mum was going into town to meet some friends. They were going to a big restaurant to have lunch.

'I think I'll wear my red dress and new earrings,'

said Mum.

They had a lovely time, and on the way home Mum decided to buy some groceries from a supermarket before she went to meet Rebecca from school. When they arrived home, Mum carried the box of groceries into the kitchen, took her coat off and put the kettle on to make a cup of tea. While the water was boiling she started to prepare the food.

'Mum,' said Rebecca as she eventually sat down, 'why are you wearing only one earring?'

Mum touched her ears with her fingers. Rebecca was right. She *was* wearing only one earring.

'Oh no!' she said. 'The other one must have fallen out somewhere. I hope I've lost it in the house and not in the street.'

Rebecca saw that her mum was very sad that she had lost her special earring.

'Finish your cup of tea, Mum,' she said kindly, 'I'll help you to look for your earring.'

Rebecca went into the hall. She looked under the rug. She did not find Mum's earring but she did find a piece of jigsaw.

'Oh good,' she said, 'that's the piece that was missing from the jigsaw I was doing last night. Now I can finish it.'

Adrian came in from school and flung his bag on the floor.

'What are you doing?' he asked. 'Cleaning the house?' Rebecca told him what had happened.

'All right,' he said, 'I'll come and help you look.' They looked in the cupboard where they hung their coats. They did not find Mum's earring but they did find a button from Dad's jacket, some conkers and a rather sticky sweet. Adrian put it into the waste bin and pushed the conkers in his trouser pockets.

They went to find Mum and told her what they had found. She was looking down the side of one armchair. She did not find the earring but she did find a wheel from Adrian's toy police car, a spaceman from his Lego set and some biscuit crumbs.

She looked down the side of the other chair. She did not find the earring but she did find two safety pins, three sweet papers and a bus ticket.

'However did *they* get down there?' she asked, puzzled.

Keith, Rebecca and Adrian's big brother, came in. 'What's the matter with Mum?' he asked. 'She looks very miserable.'

'She's lost one of her special earrings,' they said, 'we can't find it anywhere.'

'I'll help you to look for it,' said Keith, 'I'll look upstairs.'

He looked everywhere. In the bathroom, in the bedrooms, under the rugs, at the side of the cupboards and under the beds. He did not find the earring, but he did find the key to his bicycle lock, a badge, and a 10p coin which Mum said he could keep for being so helpful.

Dad came home.

'You all look very miserable tonight,' he said. 'What's wrong?' Keith, Rebecca and Adrian all

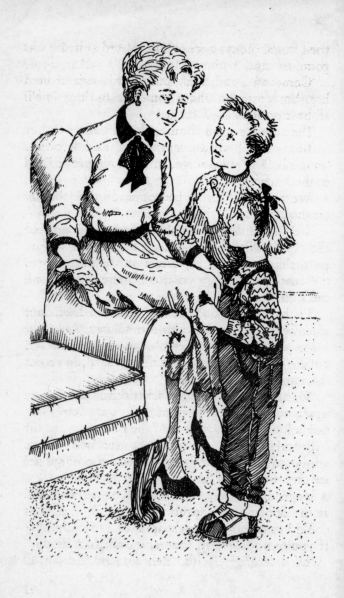

tried to tell him at once. Mum looked as if she was going to cry.

'Come on,' said Dad, putting his arm around her shoulders, 'let's have some tea and then we'll all have another look for it.'

'I'm sure it's in the house,' Mum said.

'But we've looked *everywhere*,' said Rebecca, 'in the hall, in the lounge, in the dining room and in the kitchen.'

'We've looked in the bedroom, on the landing, on the stairs and in the bathroom,' added Keith.

'We've found lots of other things,' Adrian told him, 'but not Mum's special earring. We've looked on the floor, under rugs, behind the sofa, down the sides of the armchairs, in cupboards and we can't think of anywhere else to look, can you?'

'I'll have a think about it,' promised Dad, 'but meanwhile I'll put these groceries away.'

He put away the vegetables and margarine and put the flour and sugar onto the shelf. Then he put the biscuits into a tin.

'Wait a minute,' he said, 'what's this?' And there in the box, on top of a tin of fruit, was Mum's lost earring.

Everybody was very happy, especially Mum, who decided that they would open a tub of special ice cream to celebrate.

Mr Henshaw, the next door neighbour, knocked at the door. 'Sorry to bother you,' he said, 'but could I borrow your newspaper for a few minutes? If you're not using it, that is,' he added politely.

'Of course,' said Dad, 'here you are.'

'You're all in a happy mood tonight,' said Mr Henshaw. 'Celebrating something special, are you? Whose birthday is it?'

They told him all about Mum losing her special earring and how happy she was now that it had been found.

'Try some of this ice cream,' said Mum. 'It's got bits of toffee in it.'

'Don't mind if I do,' said Mr Henshaw. 'You know,' he said, 'this reminds me of that story Jesus told, about the woman who lost a precious silver coin. She was so upset that she almost turned the house upside down until she found it.'

'I know how she felt,' said Mum. 'It's horrible when you think you've lost something special but it's lovely when you find it again.'

'Our vicar once told us that Jesus used the story as a picture of the way God feels about all of us,' said Mr Henshaw. 'Because we are so special to him it makes him very sad when we do wrong things, but when we go back and say "sorry" it makes him very, very happy.'

'He must love us very much,' said Rebecca.

'Yes,' said Mr Henshaw, 'I'm sure he does.'